While I'm waiting

By

TAMIKO JACKSON-GREGORY

Copyright © 2020 While I'm Waiting

All rights reserved. No part of this publication may be reproduced, distributed, or transmitted in any form or by any means, including photocopying, recording, or other electronic or mechanical methods, without the prior written permission of the publisher, except in the case of brief quotations embodied in critical reviews and certain other noncommercial uses permitted by copyright law.

Published February 1, 2021

Crystal Clear Publishing

www.crystalclearpublishing.us

Thank You

I want to first thank God for without Him, none of this would have been possible!

To my girls, my babies; Brittney, Makayla, and Kennedy. I love you girls so much; you girls are my world, and you mean so much to me. This is not just my story, but you too have gone through this journey along with me, but in your own way. It amazes me that when I thought you were not strong enough and I felt I needed to hold you up. You three in turn showed me your strength and carried me at times. I love you girls with my whole heart!!

To my loving and supportive parents, Benjamin and Beverly, thank you for just being there and all your love and support. Thank you for your listening ear and putting what I needed first above all else to make sure that we would be ok. I love and cherish you both.

To my Jackson family, words cannot express how much I love and appreciate you all. From every word of encouragement, every act of love, to wanting to do what you wanted to do to "handle it" (lol) I'm forever grateful. Thank you, thank you, thank you!!

They say it takes a village and it definitely does. I appreciate each and every one of you for all that have done and every push, pat on the back, all the love and support. Every call, text, visit and most importantly your prayers. I love you all so very much!

To every Pastor, Minister and Leader that has taken the time to comfort me, pray with and for me and answer my every phone call. I will never forget what you all have done for me. I cannot name you all, but you know who you are. I love you and I thank you tremendously.

To my Spiritual father and Bishop, J.Q. Smith. It is so much that can be said about your guidance, prayers, and wisdom that helped me get through some of the worst moments in my life. You became a part of my life while I was transitioning if I can say that. I was in what I would call the second trimester of my birthing experience. I had no idea where I was going and what was going to happen, but you kept reminding me of who God is and you would walk me through every single step from then on. You called me daughter from the very beginning and that is something that I will never forget. You push me, you challenge me, you even correct me when I'm wrong and show me the right way "the next time." To think that this book and title all came from an assignment that you gave me to complete. I cherish every single conversation and every teaching moment that is given. Pastor Robin would be so proud to know that we have connected. I love you, Lady Jasmine, and the entire Birthing Worship Cathedral Family!

Thank you, Crystal, and Atenya of Crystal Clear Publishing, for all that you have done to bring my vision to life. I was nervous about what I was doing and from the first meeting I left with a feeling of excitement and confidence to move forward. Thank You!

Foreword

But they who wait for the Lord shall renew their strength;

They shall mount up with wings like eagles; they shall run and not be weary; they shall walk and not faint.

Isaiah 40:31

These provoking words of the prophet Isaiah teaches us that waiting is an option, but it is not for the faint or the weary. We all have been through a waiting season or will go through one at some point of life. It is how you we persevere through these seasons that matters the most. Waiting is defined by dictionary.com as the action of staying where one is or delaying action until a particular time or until something else happens.

Many times, we have wondered, if we serve a sovereign God; why does his beloved have to wait? Waiting is a tool that God uses to define and equip us for what he has called us too. It is in that season, that we find our true identity, and the places God needs to define the most. I believe Pastor Tamiko is the right person to teach us the principles and show us what to do and what not to do while we wait.

While I'm Waiting is a life changing and brave book in which she weaves together her wisdom with personal experiences. I believe each page will give you a principle that help you on your journey of waiting and becoming who God has called you to be. So, open your hearts to receive what God has downloaded in this book just for you.

Daughter, I believe this is just the beginning of many to come. Continue to be open and transparent because this is what we need in this hour. I trust the God in you and thank you for including my words in your charge.

+Bishop JeQuavian Q. Smith

Contents

Chapter 1: Count It All Joy 1

Chapter 2 What The Hell 7

Chapter 3: The Stretching 18

Chapter 4: The Manifestation 26

Chapter 5: My Yes 36

Chapter 6: He Was There All The While 44

Chapter 7: False Labor 55

Chapter 8: The Lie 62

Chapter 9: It Was Good That I Was Afflicted 73

Chapter 10: While I'm Waiting 80

Chapter 1

COUNT IT ALL JOY

The Bible tells us that we should count it all joy when we fall into divers' temptations, because it is the trying and testing of our faith. We are to let patience have her perfect work so that we may be perfect and entire, wanting nothing. Sometimes you wonder if there is an exception to the rules when you are going through something that feels like it will rip your heart apart. I went back and did a little digging into the passages that suggests such things. In the book of James, chapter 1 verses 2 through 8, James goes in a little deeper:

My brethren count it all joy when ye fall into divers' temptations, knowing this, that the trying of your faith worketh patience. But let patience have her perfect work, that ye may be perfect and entire, wanting nothing. If any of you lack wisdom, let him ask of God, that giveth to all men liberally, and upbraideth not; and it shall be given him. But let him ask in faith, nothing wavering. For he, that wavereth is like a wave of the sea driven with the wind and tossed. For let not that man think that he shall receive any thing of the Lord. A double minded man is unstable in all his ways.

James discusses the trials of life and the various testing and tribulations of a Christian. Although no one wants to be tested and placed in the fire of adversity, it is suggested that we are to accept these adversities with great joy. Often when going through these tests and trials it often makes us bitter, not better and when that happens there tends to be no spiritual growth. Now understand that God does not send trials, but He does allow them to happen. It is though our own lust and desires that brings these trials to pass. Through these trials, James assures us that the trying "approving" of our faith worketh patience. The question is, will we stand and endure, or will we give up and walk away? I believe that God allows trials and tribulations to mature His people, such pressure produces rich benefits such as endurance and patience. James states that **When** we fall and not **If** we are going to fall into diverse temptations it is used to produce patience. The Greek work for Patience is ***Hupomone*** which means to remain under; ***hupo*** (under) and ***meno*** (to stay, abide, or remain). Patience is among the many qualities that the Spirit of God develops in the life of the believer.

Galatians 5:22-23, *But the fruit of the Spirit is love, joy, peace, long-suffering, gentleness, goodness, faith, meekness, temperance: against such there is no law.*

Fruit that is produced in the believer is significant for several reasons. (1) It means the result, product, outcome, or effect is produced by the Spirit in the believer's life. (2) As fruit on a tree takes time to grow and mature, it is the same process with the fruits of the Spirit, these virtues do not cultivate in the believer's life overnight. Patience is a quality characteristic that is developed in/within the believer as they learn to deal with people and circumstances that test, try or annoy them. Now understand, that when James tells us to count it all joy, he knows that we will not be joyful all the time in the trial, but I do believe that he was saying that count it all joy is a faith response.

I was studying these verses while writing about waiting patiently until the manifestation of whatever it was that God was doing in my life in this particular season. My prayer was that God do more in my life and take me to the place where He wanted me to be, but I don't believe that I was ready for what was to come. I heard a preacher say once, that hope deferred maketh the heart sick, but when the desire comes it is like the tree of life. In a season of waiting for the trial to be over, the hope delayed made my heart sick due to uncertainty and waiting for my expected end. Not only was I enduring the trial and all that it came with, but the possible pain of such trials and waiting was the hardest thing for me to endure especially when trying to encourage myself.

Have you ever had a moment where someone else was going through something and you had all the right things to say to encourage them, pray for them, and felt like you had reached God on their behalf? Then when it is time to encourage yourself it is like you are lost for words and it even seems as if it takes a lot of work to not only hear what you're saying but believing it. I was on an emotional rollercoaster all the time, one minute I was encouraging myself, dancing, rejoicing and even hosting girls' night, but as soon as the next "hit" came along I was asking God, Did He see what was happening to me? Where was He? I just knew God was gonna show up any given moment. I was looking for the wrath of God to come and strike them down. As funny as that sound I was just looking for some type of sign or evidence that God was fighting for me. I wanted to see the fall and demise of my enemies, but as we all know it does not work that way. I would read over and over the encouraging scriptures, praying and fasting more than I ever had before. I would cry out to the Lord, because with my natural eyes I could not see Him moving on my behalf. I was exhausted from waking up at 3am most mornings to pray, then getting back up to have the girls to school at 7:45am. I believed that I was praying and fasting for the reconciliation of my marriage, but God was doing something else in me.

One day I was reading in Jeremiah and I went to chapter 29, verses 11-14. I kept reading those scriptures over and over because I wanted to have a full understanding of what God was saying to me. The one thing that I kept hearing was that He was going to bring me out of this and place me back to where I was held captive, that I will have peace and if I called upon Him, He would hearken unto me. I had that all in my heart and waiting on the day that I would be released and returned to my place of peace. Then I read verse 13 and what stood out to me was when it stated that we (I) shall seek him and find Him. He also said, "When ye shall search for me with all of your heart." Just that little significant piece of scripture had me thinking and naturally I asked what He was trying to tell me. How was I to seek Him with my whole heart? How do I do this? He told me to remove everything that does not align itself with Him and put it aside and focus on Him and Him alone. Remove all hurt, anger, malice, pettiness, and my pride. He said, "Search for ME, Look for ME, and I will give you the peace that surpasses all your understanding. I began to cry, and I walked away from the table, took of my glasses, and walked over to my living room and began to worship as I walked my hardwood floors. I worshiped until my heart was empty and all I wanted was for God to fill it with nothing but Him. Worship for me prior to going into prayer is a way that I feel, sets me in an atmosphere where I can reach God with such a presence that I never want to leave.

I made up in my mind that in this season of my life that all I wanted to do was give Him my YES! No matter what I was going through and no matter how much pain I was in and who walked away, I was still going to give Him my YES! My song of encouragement in my time of despair and grieving, was *Yes,* by *Shekinah Glory.* I just wanted to again give my absolute Yes! I felt like if this is what I got to go through then I'm going to go through it the best way I know how, flaws and all. I shall call upon the Lord and go and pray and He will listen to me. While I'm Waiting!

Chapter 2

WHAT THE HELL

W*hat the Hell!!!!* I always said that if I were to write a book, I would start my first sentence with this one phrase. I began writing in my journal on November 14th in 2017 at 6:21am. I used this journal to track my dreams and visions that I felt the Lord had given to me. I would leave a blank page so that I could write the purpose or the meaning of said dream/vision at a later time. I labeled this journal *My Dream Catcher*, but it ended up being the one thing that kept me sane and giving me a release when things would seem to be too heavy to carry. I expressed my hurt, anger, pain, and regret all in this one place that I felt safe and no one would know but me and God. I started out writing 3 and 4 pages with each entry and every feeling that I had ever felt, was placed in it. This lasted for a while until I only had 1 or 2 pages to fill. Never would I have imagined that my Dream Catcher would be a book in the making.

I began to think about my life, right at this moment and how I ended up here. Don't worry I am no longer angry nor am I bitter, I believe that I mastered those feelings some time ago. I will be honest and let you know that there are times when those feelings do surface from time to time. Between fasting, praying and my therapist, I believe that I have learned to deal with the five stages of grief a lot better. You know **Denial, Anger, Bargaining, Depression and then Acceptance**. I was in great denial, because I could not believe that I; me of all people, was going through a separation let alone a divorce. I mean, this has happened to so many people that I knew but ME, US, Nah!! I am not saying that I am exempt, but this took me by absolute surprise. Where did all this come from and why was this happening? Bargaining was my best friend, I made so many promises to the Lord. "Oh God if you would just... I'll ....," I was willing to do whatever was needed to be done if God would just fix it. All I wanted was for God to fix whatever was broken and whatever other issues we had counseling would fix the rest. We tend to bargain with God just as we do with people to get what it is that we want, and I desperately wanted my marriage to be fixed. That word "fix" has so many meanings to only consist of three letters. They all come together to have the same meaning; to secure, position, settle, mend or repair. That is exactly what I thought I wanted, a quick fix. All those words mean is that I would have still been in the same position or place with no change. The only thing that would have changed is the pretty patch over wounds that were left open, and I would have been settling, stagnant in something with no real change. What I mean is that he carried past and present issues and needed more than I had to give, and I was dealing with my own insecurities and frustrations. We tend to love our significant others or people in general so much that there are times when we can't see what's right in front of us or just love them past those things.

Depression and anxiety caused me to hide in my room and no appetite to eat like I normally would. My routine consisted of early morning prayer and most mornings I would walk for a few miles prior to getting the girls up for school. I could only eat a boiled egg or two and maybe a piece of fruit and water. Full meals would make me nauseous and this went on for quite some time. I went from crying all throughout the day to crying only in the shower so the kids wouldn't hear me and feel the need to comfort me as they too were hurting. My anxiety was so bad that if I saw his call come across my phone screen, my heart would feel like it was about to jump out of my chest. It wasn't until one morning I was getting ready to shower after a 3-mile walk, that I just let the phone ring, because I could not allow him to call me with another thing that was taking the little peace that I did have. I had done everything to make my living space livable and got rid of everything that reminded me of him in the bedroom we once shared. On one of her visits, my mom sat on my bed and suggested that I do something to make my room more like me. This was after my husband had been gone for some time and all of his belongings were removed from the bedroom. I went online after deciding on the colors that I wanted my bedroom to be. I had decided to change my colors from cream and burgundy to gray and yellow. I found everything I needed, and I began to make the necessary changes and even stretched out my clothing in the walk-in closet where his clothes once hanged. I ordered black out curtains to keep the room "cool" and yellow sheers to go in the middle, but I kept the curtains closed more than open because I wanted to stay in my dark safe place.

I would smile on the outside and cry on the inside. I had to do a lot of hiding my real emotions from my friends, family, and most of all my girls. Not because I didn't want them to see me at a weak or vulnerable time, but because they carried my pain as well as their own. So, I took advantage of my shower time and their time away visiting and at school. One morning after I got the girls off to school, I came home and crawled back into my bed. My mom came over walked into my room, opened my curtains, and told me to get up out of the bed, but as soon as she headed to the kitchen to make me breakfast. I got up closed my blinds, shut my curtains, and flopped back into the bed. My room was constantly dark and that is how I liked it, because I was comfortable. All I wanted to do at times was be alone in my bubble, but that bubble that I was in had memories of what we shared together. I would have a Girls Night just about every weekend, when the girls were away to have company, eat seafood, sip, and talk about our different situations. I did not mind being alone, but I found that girl's night was helping me to forget about my situation, even for a little while. Honestly, it took me almost a little over a year to gain acceptance. I will explain my acceptance later...

It all began after a full day of dealing with the girls and getting them settled in from school and getting all homework done, it is now time for dinner and getting them ready for bed. I have had a few calls from him throughout the day, which was normal, but around 10pm on this particular night, my life changed forever. I received a phone call that would change my way of life as I knew it. Never in a million years did I expect to hear this on the other end, "I met someone, and we have been talking and seeing each other for about week now." Now in my mind I am wondering when did this happened? I mean we were just on a cruise not even a week ago, so this must have been immediate. He began to explain how they met and that she had been coming by his place of employment to see him. I had a lot of questions, but nothing could have stopped the tears from flowing from my eyes. We talked off and on until about 1am and I was finally able to get some sleep or the lack there of due to my anxiety and stomach knotting so badly. After a few days of talking and trying to keep things as normal as possible for the girls it was becoming the most difficult thing, we both had to do. Even in all that hiding and pretending, the girls were watching, and they knew that something was not right.

I had just opened my very own salon 3 or 4 months prior. It had been a dream of mine since I was a little girl. This very weekend after I was told about the other woman, I was preparing the salon for its' very first event, I was hosting my first Pop-Up Shop. That Friday prior to the event I was locking up my salon and I just happen to look to my left, and I see the police vehicle car sitting in the open parking area. Being new to that area of the city, I did not know that the police frequent that area all the time to sit, talk or watch as we close at night. I immediately heard in my ear, "she's an officer." Now I am flipping out because I know this chic is not sitting at my place of business. I get home and while we were sitting at the dining room table waiting on our Pastor friends to talk with us, I ask, "Is she and officer?" He looks at me like how you knew. My response was, "The Lord told me!" I went back and thought about how he explained to me how they met because it seems just a little too simple to me. I had begun to narrow it down for him. I said, "Now is she a Garden City Officer?" He responded, "No." I said, "Well it couldn't be one of Savannah's Officers, being the place where he met her, and she had just gotten off." I am not sure where it came from, but I said, "There is only one last option so she must be a Port Officer!" I nailed it ladies and gentlemen because the facial expression told it all.

I began to ask questions like, did she know who I was and where I worked and he stated, "No!" Sidebar…Now ladies we know that was a bold face lie!! God made women beautiful and most defiantly smart and we can find out more information than the CIA by using a piece of gum, a pen, and a computer within a 5-minute span. The gum is for us to chew to keep us calm as our fingers move 100 mph on our computer keypads or on our cell phones. All I had to do was go under his Facebook page and see recently added friends and there she was. Now looking through her profile I knew about as much as I needed to know about who she was for the time being. This girl had already known who I was, where I worked, my babies names and probably what color nail polish I was wearing in no time, but some men don't think!! One thing I always told my kids and my husband, I might seem a little slow or I might not catch it right then and there, but I am so much smarter than a fifth grader and eventually, I will catch it.

November 14, 2017 6:21am

This is the absolute hardest thing that I have ever had to write in my life. I wish this were a dream, but in reality, it is not. With almost 15 years of marriage, I will be separated from my husband. Although things of this sort happen all the time, I never saw this happening to us....

This was the very first entry in the *Dream Catcher* since this all began. Don't get me wrong, I am a confident woman, and I was raised by some of the strongest women I know, and they taught me a great deal when it came to men and marriage. I was tough at times and I felt that somewhere down the line I messed up, was not good enough, or was not fast enough. I had to go through the holidays alone for the first time in 16 years. We were together a little over a year before getting married, so this was new to me not having him to celebrate the holidays. Our 15-year anniversary was in December and I was spending what was supposed to be a celebration, in Augusta, Ga with my aunt. Not to mention Christmas was not the same because he did not want to get the girls unless they were coming to his new place of residence to meet his new. My question was why you would want to break the news to the girls on Christmas, that you have left their mother for someone else. It wasn't until the 28th of December that he finally made his way to spend time with them for Christmas. The girls enjoyed riding their new bikes in the park and spending time with their father.

Upon their return home I was summonsed outside to talk with my husband. His phone rang and it was her…I politely asked that he not answer her, and he told me he had to. Now I'm thinking that's cool that you talk to her but at least show me the proper respect as I am still your wife. I was asked by him to come outside, in the cold, and the only thing I asked for was a little respect. Well, he answered her after he missed the first call, so I walked off and headed for the front door. He was right behind me telling me he needed to get his files from inside of the house. I shut the door in his face and locked it behind me, next thing I know my mom let him in the house. I came flying out of my room and next thing I know I walked over to the desk where is files were located and took the container of files and flung them onto the porch. Now I don't know when he moved out my way, because all I could see was red, he left and went and sat in his car. All I can tell you was that whatever was buried in me had surfaced and a side of me that I had never seen before showed up. I went back to the same spot and grabbed the file cabinet and flung it too (that file cabinet was not light either). "Ni Come Get It!!" I yelled, with a side of I wish you would! Listen, I'm laughing so hard right now, but I was crazy in that moment, but I bet you one thing…he stayed in that car. I'm not glorifying what I did or how I acted, because my two younger babies were right there, and they were crying. I had to calm myself down and then apologize not only to them, but to my mother as well. Thank God that he didn't take those files because they contained some very important information that I needed later down the road.

Sometime in January it began to snow, and I was again feeling some type of way, because we all loved playing in the snow. It was a big deal because here in Savannah we don't get snow like that. After taking videos of the girls playing in the snow, the depression hit me once again. I sat up in the bed and I decided to call my Mentor on the phone, and I told her all that had been going on with me and my marriage. She was so loving and at the same time she reminded me that God always sends us warning before something happens. He did, twice! The dream that I had happened the exact same way both times, and I believe that they were about a year or so apart. I never thought anything more about it because I was secure in my marriage, he was my husband, my lover and most importantly my best friend. If I had written it in my journal it would go like this:

Date: Unknown

This was the strangest dream that I have ever had. I dreamt that I was driving and while doing so the tears filled my eyes. I ended up at my Mentors house. I drove through the gate and down the long dirt road to her house. When I pulled up to her house, I saw her sitting at the table on her deck. I walked up to her and fell on my knees and placed my head in her lap and cried. She asked me what was wrong, and I told her that he had left me and said that he found someone else. She let me cry it out and gave me some encouraging words and prayed with me and I returned home. I don't know what this means, but I shook it off because we said that we would get though anything, and we were looking forward to growing old together.

Chapter 3

THE STRETCHING

I attended church services as I usually did on Sunday's. After service was over, I was talking to some friends and one of the Ministers came up to me and asked if her and her husband could pray with and for me. I was hesitant at first because I had so much going on and I just wanted to shut off the smiles and the funny, joking self that I normally am. I allowed them to do so and one of them said, "I keep hearing the Lord say Patience." He said that I had to be patient in this season and wait on God. The other Minister told me that she saw me praying and speaking and fire was coming from my mouth. Now being that I am a little weary of the things people tell me, "thus said the Lord" I accepted the prayer and went home. Sometime later I understood more and more to what they were saying. With anything that needs attention, I took all the Word that had been given to me and all that I had read over time and started putting it to work and doing research. I researched scriptures, read books and anything that had to do with Spiritual Warfare. I read several scriptures for patience and I chose a few to study and got familiar with them. In Galatians it tells us not to be weary in well doing, because at the proper time we are going to reap the if we do not give up. It is only a matter of time before we will reap the divine reward if we keep going.

You know when you are going through something and you watch shows and different things on television, it seems as if it is directly in comparison to your situation. I would watch TBN all during the day and late at night and it seemed as if John Gray, Steven Furtick, Joyce Meyers and TD Jakes all had messages that was just for me and somehow spoke directly to my situation. I remember John Gray had a sermon that he was preaching, and he was talking about the man leaving his family for another woman. I was praying that my husband was listening, but it was 2 in the morning, so I knew better. He began to talk about the spirits associated with this type of behavior and we all have heard it but was never really taught on in depth. What is this spirit that I speak of Jezebel! It was a word that was commonly laughed at on the sitcom Sanford, when Esther would call the loose women on the show. Now that I have experienced it, it is not so funny to me anymore, it's more depressing than anything because I have experienced it firsthand.

I pulled myself up by my bootstraps and decided to do a little homework. I googled and read anything and everything that I could on the Jezebel spirit. I came across an article written by Michael Bradley called the *Jezebel Spirit and How it Operates*. I spent a few days reading the 14 pages because during the time of my grieving, a lot of the information was hard to digest. The article broke down exactly what the Jezebel spirit is and the things that it does to an individual and how it operates. This spirit is considered much more evil, cunning and it is harder to deal with once it attaches itself to a person. The article goes on and on, but the aftermath of the spirit was the part that made it so difficult to digest. "I have seen this spirit literally play some people right over the edge of a cliff where they ended up losing everything. And this was all because they were too blind and ignorant to see what was really going on behind the scenes in the spiritual realm." (M. Bradley). After the individual has lost everything, the 'Host" begins to attack the individual. Meaning it will play mind games, attacking the self-esteem of the individual, and self-confidence. Prophet Elijah was so distraught after coming in contact with Queen Jezebel and the spirit that was in her that he wanted to give up and quit until God gave him strength and an angel gave him a word from the Lord.

Those that sow to his flesh will reap what he has sown. This has been this way from the beginning of time, so God what was taking so long? I'm still in Galatians and when Paul wrote this, he was not supporting a law of spiritual karma, but he relates these principles of reaping and sowing to the way conduct we ourselves.

Many would tell me that during in this season I was being Broken, Stretched and Birthing something! I did not want to hear that at times, because I wanted it but not like this. Joyce L. Rodgers visited my former church during a Sunday service, and she preached about being stretched.

She said, "A rubber band is stretched to hold the capacity of a thing. Many of you are being stretched in this season. Know that God is stretching you to increase your capacity to receive. After the stretching comes the blessing." It took me an awfully long time to accept what I was going through. I thought if I made changes, read a book on Forgiveness by Joyce Meyers, pray harder, or recite the words of confessions from my confession book, God would give me my expected end quickly. When they say that hope maketh the heart sick, there were not lying. This meant that I had more praying and work to do, being that I was coming to grips to what was happening to my family. Just as I did with the Jezebel spirit, I did with the birthing, stretching and being broken. I am one that must get in the word and look things up so that I will know exactly what it is that I am talking about or what is being said. Now if there was something that I still did not understand, I had a few Ministers that I was able to turn to for guidance and support. Being that I was being stretched it was one of the first words that I looked up. I did not forget what was already said about the rubber band when it is stretched. I just wanted to go a little further and a little deeper trying to understand what was happening to me.

God stretches us and our trust in Him, because He already knows what is that we are in need of even before we ask. In my case I felt like I was being stretched, but at the same time I was so broken that I could not and would not accept that this thing was happening to me. He was bending me in ways that I did not know was possible, but He did not let me break. Even in those times where I felt like I could not take it anymore. There were many days that I felt like I was going to lose the very mind that many prayed for me not to lose. I felt like everything that could happen, was happening to me. Things that I could have never imagined happening from someone who at one point treated me like the Queen that I am. All the while of going through all this hurt and pain, I had a friend of mine come to the house to ask me a question about her hair. The conversation took a turn to us discussing her marriage. I'm thinking to myself, "Now Lord I don't have much to tell her because I'm in the thick of my situation, so how can I help her?" I asked God to remove me out of the way and allow whatever it is that I say to her not come from a place of my flesh. Not long after that I had another young lady come to me about her marriage and what they were going through. I made up in my mind that if this is what I am called to do, then I'll do it. Lord just give me the strength to do so and the wisdom to do it with integrity.

Even in my brokenness I was reminded that the Lord is near to those that have a broken heart and a contrite spirit. I was broken hearted and I could not understand where God was in my situation and what was to become of this. I did not understand how God could allow this to happen to not only me, but my children are suffering as well. As a parent we want do whatever it is necessary to protect our children and keep them safe from harm. How was I going to get through this when I feel so alone, it did not matter how many people that I had in my corner, I was alone. I did everything that I could think of to encourage myself and give my babies a sense of security, even in my insecurities. I was still struggling with being patient and waiting until God's manifestation in my marriage. I knew that in due time God would manifest himself to me, but it is all in His timing.

When going through any trial, you will not be perfect and do everything the right way, but God is faithful to His word. He does, however, expects us to love others and have faith in Him as well as demonstrate obedience to said commandments. You're going to make mistakes and do things that you never thought that you would do. Remember, we all go through things, but no one, I mean absolutely no one can tell you how you should feel when going through it. We all deal in our own way and we have to figure out how to get through it. I put my kids and myself in therapy and I must admit that it helps a lot to sit and get those things out. I thought that I didn't need it because I know how to pray, and I fought with the idea. It was wonderful for the girls, but not for me, until I sat in my first session and realized that, yes, I need this as well.

BREATHE!! There will be times when you are going to go left even when you were instructed to go right. I can admit that I had my moments of cutting up and I was very ugly with it most times. I was a woman that was hurt and angry and there were times that I felt backed into a corner and I had to defend myself, because in most cases it was two against one. Never in my wildest dreams would I have seen this happening to me and being treated the way that I was. To top it off he was allowing someone else to chime in and disrespect me as well. Those that were close to me would say that I was being too quiet and not defending myself, but I was too tired at times to fight back, but when I did…I did. I was also trying to let God know that I was trying to do and be all that I could the right way and allow Him time to deal with those that were causing my hurt.

How many of us can be real and admit that sometimes God takes His time, and you need Him to bring the wrath NOW!! I was like Madea and I need them to get got because I was the one that was getting all the getting. I will tell you this, when I did take matters into my own hands at times, I would have a hard time sleeping and I would be the one being chastised. Why would I be in "trouble" you asked because I knew better, and God had already given me instruction on how to handle them. I got off track a little because I had to let them know that I was not soft or allow someone to come for me (if you will). Well while they got the message that I will not just let you handle me, I was tossing and turning because I was not supposed to say anything, and I did the direct opposite. Some of you may not know something about me and I feel that I should explain it to you. I am hard on myself at times and I am grateful that I am because it helps me to stay in line. I do not just do things and not look at how the Father would view it. Yes, I am human, but I do not let that be a get out of jail free card to do what I want and then make excuses for it. That is just me and the way I am…. I'm Still Waiting!!

Chapter 4

THE MANIFESTATION

When you are believing what God says in His word and you hear all that He is saying to you, what happens when it is not what you think He is saying. I am just realizing that all that He said to me through prophecy, reading the Bible and what he shared with me through my prayer time had absolutely nothing to do with reviving my marriage. Everything that I had been hearing and the things that God had been speaking to me started happening in 2018. I remember the first revelation came in the month of January. I was invited to a Pastoral Ordination of a friend and I had to drive to Pt. Wentworth to get to the service. I invited two others to come along with me to show our support to our sister in Christ. The whole time I am driving, I am looking to see what I could see because I had this feeling that I just could not shake.

The service was beautiful, and this was the first encounter with the Pastor of this church who is now my current Pastor and Bishop. He called for those that wanted prayer and at first, I was hesitant, because I already had several in my ear telling me this and that. I decided after a few minutes to go get in line and he asked me what my prayer was, and I told him. He prayed for me and spoke something to my spirit and not in it. I was grateful for that because I needed my spirit to be spoken to and not another prophecy told to me. After he was done, he said that I would see the manifestation of my situation within seven days. We hung around after service to speak to our newly ordained friend who is now a Pastor and of course, we needed to figure out what we were going to eat for dinner. They were going for seafood, but me and my crew decided that we were going to do something a little simpler, plus we did not feel like going downtown and dealing with the flow of River Street. I was still feeling the high from the service and after we left, I was still feeling the churn in my belly from the prayer and the feeling I had before. On the drive home I kept looking and looking, because I had this feeling that if I saw what I was looking for, it was not going to be good. We got to the restaurant and I could not even eat because I was looking at everyone that walked through the door to see if what I was feeling was true. My husband at the time was out of town so I knew that I was not going to run into him at all so if that is what you are thinking…think harder. We sat at the table and continued to laugh and enjoy each other and after we were done with dinner, we all got into my car and headed back to my house.

The kids left with their father the following morning which was a Saturday, and they were to return on that Sunday evening. Prior to them returning home Kayla called to ask about a pair of shoes being given to her and she wanted to know if it was ok to accept. I told her no thank you and that I would take them to get new sneakers soon.

Upon the girl's arrival home, they each had a bag of snacks and Kay had clothing in her bag as well. She stated that the bag contained the sneakers that I already said no to and a few jackets. I took the bag and gave it back to their father and told him no thank you. I did not want anything that belonged to his girlfriend in my house, but of course he saw no issue with Kayla bringing home another woman's garments to wear as if it was normal. I advised that he could take them back or I could throw then in the trash, needless to say, he took them back.

Prior to the argument taking place, I was in a meeting with my good friend and big sister Terry, we were going over business ideas and upcoming events for my salon. While I was outside arguing with my husband about the items in Kayla's bag, my cell was in the house and I was receiving another call from LaVita. It was not just about the clothing and shoes that was given to Kayla after I said no, but once again I was being disrespected and what I said did not matter. I had already known why she sent the garments to the house after I said no, but that was not going to get to me, because in the end the items would have been gone voluntarily or involuntarily by way of the trash can. Also, I believe wholeheartedly that spirits transfer and I did not want anything that belonged to her in my house. After I completed my meeting with Terry, she gave me some words of encouragement to calm me down from the argument that had taken place outside. After getting the girls and myself ready for bed, I took the time to call LaVita back to see what was going on and to make sure that all was well with her. When she answered, she let me know that her daughter had a message for me, and she wanted to tell me what God had given her. She said, "Remember I told you that my daughter was going on a retreat with her church." I told her yes and she proceeds to tell me that her daughter had something to tell me.

Her daughter began to tell me that while she was away on the retreat the Lord told her these words, "The Lord says not argue with your husband anymore. Do not argue with him because..." She began to reveal what the Lord was saying, but I am not going to reveal it right now. Now I know that you are like, wait some stuff was left out! I can't tell you everything, because as of right now that particular thing has happened, and I take no joy in it. LaVita returned to the phone and I began to tell her about that Friday that we had gone to the Ordination and what the Pastor had said to me and what I was feeling from that night.

They say that God protects babies and fools... Well, I'm no baby! I called my best friend, who was and is just as crazy as I am. I knew my husband was out of town again, so I was gonna just help God out a little bit and maybe He would move quicker in restoring my marriage. I drove to my friend Beck house and jumped in her car, because her car was unrecognizable, and the tint was dark. We drove past the house where she and my husband were living at a few times and there was a car there that I didn't recognize. We finally parked at a center and after some time sitting there waiting, we saw the car that was at the house drive by. We decided to go by the house again, because at this point, I was trying to see all that I can. We turned the corner past the house and who comes flying, I mean flying to the corner.... yep. We did a quick turnaround because this chick made a left and not a right to go home. It wasn't even 5 seconds to turn around and we made the left turn... What the hell? Where was she? This dog on girl has disappeared into thin air almost. Beck looked left and I was looking right, I know we both wear glasses but dang. It was dark and finally she slammed on breaks because we hit a dead end. I know she couldn't have seen me because the tint was too dark on Beck's truck. By the time we drove around another corner and passing the house once again, she had already returned home, and we missed her. We returned back to my car in absolute disbelief and confused as to what just happened. We laughed so hard on the way back to my car because it was so unbelievable. Once I got in my car, I called my mom, and you would not believe how much trouble I got in. I'm a grown woman out here and my mom was going off on me about my little adventure. She was right though, I had no business going over there and what if I did see anything, what was I gonna do with the information anyway? What good would it have done to see, if anything, was going on. After talking to my mom, I grabbed something to eat and called LaVita.... needless to say, she had a mouthful for me as well, she understood why I was doing it, and still agreeing that it wasn't worth it to have done it. I still thought it was funny no matter how much they fussed at me, but wrong on so many levels, because I knew better. I just thought I would give God some help that's all! (roll eyes).

After my adventure began a series of dreams and revelations that God had given me concerning my marriage and my husband. I wrote them all down and here it is two years later, and I am seeing that those dreams are coming to pass. The more of our friends and associated who heard about our separation and the reasons behind it, I was comforting them more than they were comforting me. There was a line of people that wanted to lay hands on them both, and I mean seriously lay hands, but it wasn't necessary. I realized that it was not me, but all the strength that I gained spent in prayer, reading my word, and fasting. There was no need to go there because God could do it better!

When God gives instructions, it is sometimes straight to the point and there will be times it will be vague. It is up to you as the individual who is in their season of waiting to ask Him for understanding or instructions. There were times when I would have full fledge conversations with God in the car, while doing the dishes, or when the spirit hit me to talk to Him. I was so lost at times and not to mention the may emotional rollercoasters that I was experiencing. I did however get to the point that I would go a full day without crying and before you knew it, I was going days, weeks, months and then I just stopped. Even on the Sunday's that I didn't have the energy to attend church, I would get up the energy to get dressed, get the kids ready, beat my face, put on a smile and make my way to church.

Date Unknown:

Two melatonin down, so why am I up at 4am on a Friday morning. The kids are not due up for school for a few hours. I was sleeping good and I thought I heard someone say II Samuel 1:15. I rolled over because no one was in the room with me, but a few minutes later I heard it again II Samuel 1:15. I shook my head yes, because I knew that I would remember to read it when I awoke so to whoever it was, I got it. I fell back asleep and this time the voice yelled it out to me as if it were saying GET UP!! II SAMUEL 1 AND 15!! I got up and I wiped my eyes and reached over to my nightstand and grabbed my bible.

And David called one of the young men, and said, go near, and fall upon him. And he smote him that he died.

Now at this point I am thinking, Lord what does that have to do with anything. I read it over and over, but still no understanding. There was no commentary at the bottom page of my bible on it, so I went to the verse before it and the verse after it. I still do not get why I had to read this scripture, but it must have had some meaning because I was awakened out of my sleep to read it. Now bear with me because this is going to take a minute explain. I called and asked a friend of mine if he could interpret the dream or break the scripture down to me and he did. He said that God was going to kill the lie! Now after he broke some things down to me, I went all the way back to the last chapter in the book of I Samuel.

Saul's son Jonathan was killed by the Philistines. David loved Jonathan and Saul very much, even though Saul tried on many occasions to kill him. You will have to go back and read the story for yourselves, but Jonathan was a great help in David's escape from his father. Later it goes on to say, because the Philistines were gaining closer to Saul, therefore Saul asked his armor-bearer to kill him because he did not want to be killed by the Philistines. His armor-bearer denied him, and Saul fell upon his own sword, the armor-bearer followed suit. Now this is where the young man came in to play. The young man was an Amalekite who came out of Saul's camp and made himself known unto David. The Amalekite was received in David's camp and eventually told David that Saul had asked him to kill him, because he did not want the Philistines to take his life. The truth is the Amalekite did not kill Saul, but he saw everything go down from the bushes or behind the scenes. This young man wanted so much to be liked or approved by David that he lied to him not knowing who Saul was to David. This is where the scripture that I was awakened for come in, David had the young man killed for taking the life of a man that he himself did not even kill. David showed Saul so much respect even when Saul treated him anyway that he saw fit. David had many opportunities to kill Saul, but he chose not to, because Saul was one of God's anointed. This Amalekite lost his life all because he lied from his own mouth about taking the life of Saul.

As you know in life, people will do whatever they need to in order to make whatever they did seem justifiable. When the original story has been changed to create another version, it doesn't always get the expected outcome they were hoping for. In most cases those that change the story, do so by taking bits and pieces of the actual story and use only what they want others to know, never telling the truth. This man had no idea that his life was gonna end, all because he wanted to be seen as honorable. There is no honor in lying to get what you want and at the cost of causing hurt to someone else. It's even more horrifying when children are involved, and you are doing the best you know how to make sure that they are gonna be okay.

Chapter 5

MY YES

Not everyone should be privy to what you are going through. I will admit that it is hard to keep some things to yourself, especially when you have such a large circle of friends and people in your life. There were times where I had to take people out of my ear, because I was literally losing it and I was so confused and tired. You would not believe some of the things that people was telling me to do and how to pray to restore my marriage. For example, I had someone tell me to pull out my marriage license and pray over it for 7 days and my marriage would be restored. Yeah, I know, Plus, I wasn't sure at that time that I wanted the marriage anymore because I was battling back and forth with my feelings. Therefore, it is so important to have trusted people in your circle, that you know who loves you and has your best interest at heart. My family had been notified after the Thanksgiving holiday and I received a lot of support and encouragement. My mother and my girls were my rock through the whole ordeal. I spoke to her every day and she came over on her days off to help me with the girls and allowed me to have time to myself by taking the girls with her or allowing me time to get out of the house.

I have this one aunt, my aunt Jerrilene, that I called just about every single day. She was very instrumental in my being able to get through all that I was enduring, basically walking me through it. I thank God for her, because she was so patient and carried me as if I was her own. Praying for both me and my husband and standing in prayer when I had no more energy to do so, to encouraging me and always reminding me of who I was to God…His daughter. I remember she used to tell me all the time that God had bottled all the tears that I cried, and He will work on my behalf. Again, I was looking for the wrath of God to happen, but it was happening but not how I was looking for it to happen. January 31, 2018 was the day that I had a realization that I needed to care about me more than I cared for my husband and what he was doing. Not even a week or two prior to this date, I had to go pick up some paperwork to review from the Mediation Center to begin the divorce proceedings, and I decided that if this were the route that I was being taken down, I had to make sure that I was doing what it took to make sure that me and my girls would be ok. Prior to Mediation papers I was told what I was gonna get, and what was gonna happen and if it wasn't enough…make it enough or get another job.

I always told God that no matter what happened, or who came and who left that I would always give Him my YES! "*God, I give you my yes, even when I cannot see it. YES, even when I cannot feel you. YES, even when it hurts me to my core, YES, No matter what God. YES!* The songs tell us that we must sometimes encourage ourselves and by saying YES! That was my way of encouraging myself. I would say yes over and over until I felt something, it was my way of gaining power and strength. It does not take long for someone who you loved, to turn into someone you never knew existed when things like this happens. Trust me, I had my moments as well, but I believe mine were more in retaliation and defense than malice. Anyway, on this day I Asked God to help me through the process and to help give me peace and acceptance as to what was happening. The one thing that I hated to hear was that my husband had free will, and God was not going to make him do anything that he did not want to do. It was a hard pill to swallow, but I got myself together and did what I had to do, because I was gonna be a single mother. I declared that I was NOT gonna go through this for nothing. "Lord I will take the loss if my children and my children's children will not have to go through this in their life, I broke every generational curse on both sides of the family, and I will take the loss if that means my children will live their life fully unto the Lord."

During my time of study, I was reminded to stand still and see the salvation of the Lord in the book of Exodus. I moved over to the book of II Corinthians the second chapter. In short from verse 6 to 10, God was saying that His punishment is sufficient for him, but not unto death, I must forgive and show love towards him as God loves and forgives me. After reading that I questioned God on forgiveness when it came to my husband and the woman that interfered in my marriage. Not that I could not do it, but did I have to do it right then and there? See there I go again, asking and bargaining with God on His word. Now God I will forgive, but I just cannot do it right now, plus I just told him a few choice words and I am not ready to forgive just yet. Not only am I being affected and going through this thing, but my girls are feeling it as well. I had one who was going through a great deal of stress until it was causing anxiety attacks on a regular basis. The middle one had so many questions and crying all the time, but she still found the strength to sing worship songs around the house to encourage herself. The baby girl felt some type of way, but never really showed her emotions too much. There was a lot of pain in the house, but at the same time there was joy as well. I was learning to accept that this was my life, and I was living it to the best of my ability. Prior to my husband leaving I had just started my weight loss journey and by this time I was slimmer and feeling myself a little bit. I got a new hair style by shaving down the left side of my head and the back. I would have the top and right side of my hair full and lifted with height. I came out of wearing so much black and added more color to my wardrobe and a little more accessories. I started dabbing in makeup a little more and later found that I was falling in love with the me that I had lost, between busy life of being a wife and mother.

I still wore my wedding rings, because I had too much going on and I did not want nor sought for male attention. Sometimes we get so caught up in life that we forget who we are. I was a wife, mother, minister, friend and over several projects in my former church. This was my opportunity to get me together and find out who I really am all over again. I was a mom at the age of 21 with my first daughter, met my husband about four years later and we were married a year and a half after meeting. Our other girls came five and seven years into our marriage, so our hands were pretty full. I worked a full-time job all the time until we agreed that I would resign in order for me to finish Cosmetology school. This also gave me the opportunity to be available to the girls because they were so young, while he worked on the Ambulance and did what was necessary to further his career. My marriage was not all bad and we had some great times and a lifetime of memories. All marriages takes work, and the work has to be done by both parties as well as the willingness to commit to working out whatever the need is. I looked through two of my other journals and found that I wanted to walk away on many occasions, but I stayed, because we were young and at times foolish in our decision making, it was my choice and one I don't regret.

Life for me was a little hectic and frustrating at times when one person is home with the kids for long periods of time. My husband was on 24-hour shifts and carried several positions throughout his career: a S.W.A.T. medic, fire fighter and a EMT instructor. It was good for me to be available with the girls more, because I had a high schooler, and the little ones were in elementary school. Attending programs and school outings were more so just me at times, but when he was available, he did show up for the girls. We did have quite a bit of family time together especially on the weekends. Our family vacations were always grand and a few times out of the year we would take "Our Time" trips together, just to get away and learn of each other again. It is funny because we realized that most of the time, we talked about the kids more than anything. One thing I have learned during this process is to value and respect the time that you have with your significant other. No matter what you experience, learn to pick your battles, and communicate more and not only communicate but get understanding. There is nothing that you can go through that cannot be worked out, especially with natural and spiritual counseling.

We opened two businesses in one week. God was moving in ways that we had never imagined. I was in a salon already and had been there for six years. A year and a half of that time I was working as the Salon Manager and I took that profoundly serious and I used it to learn how to run my very own salon. We would have meetings twice a year to go over the bills and the running of that salon and any issues that we had going on. After some time, I felt like I was able to carry a salon on my own and that was what I was going to do. He worked out of the house with his clients that needed CPR certification and more. We discussed trying to find a building large enough to operate both businesses out of. Thank God that did not happen! I found my building first and it was right around the corner from the salon that I was currently working in. It was perfect and the landlord was so sweet and although he did not want another salon to open in that space, due to past history. He allowed me to come in and open, because he said there was something about me that was giving him a good feeling. To this day, almost three years later, I am still standing. Sometime later my husband found a building that was perfect for him and business was coming in left and right for him and he was still working as a fire fighter and an EMT instructor at one of the local colleges.

There are many facets as to why all of this took place, but I do know that the words that we speak are honored. One Sunday I was going through something and I felt like I just wanted to be so closed to God that I did not want anything to come in between what was happening. I wrote a list of things that I wanted God to do in my life and the life of my family and as I look back on that list, He was doing just that. I remember going to the alter at my former church and I told God that I wanted more of Him and I wanted to go to the next level, "Even if He had to remove my husband to do it." Now listen, before you oooh and aahh and say how bold I was to ask this, just listen. We had already begun to go through some things, and I saw within a year before some of the things that we wanted in life were totally different. I felt that we were together but going in two different paths. I am not saying I was perfect, and I cannot say what he wanted and did not want, but there were times where even I thought about leaving. So, because I had made my request known to God, of course this is what happened, but I never expected to happen this way. Maybe it was the wrong thing to say, but hey, I said it. We have to be careful what we say out of our mouths, even when it sounds good. We ask but never know how God is gonna do it and what we have to go through to get it! From then on even when the preacher says, "Tell your neighbor" I am leery about repeating it, lol. While I'm Waiting!

Proverbs 16:23

Wisdom is shown by what we speak and controlling the words that come from our mouths. Wisdom is evident where it teaches the mouth what and what not to say!

Chapter 6

HE WAS THERE ALL THE WHILE

While you are in that waiting season, what are you doing? How are you handling the situation that you are going through? These are the questions that most people do not know how to answer. Although I was one to encourage and be there for others in need, I had no earthly idea how to handle my waiting season. Now I have said earlier that I fasted, prayed, cried, and got angry, but what do you do in that down time, when no one is around, or you have to go about your normal life. There are so many books to read and advise from loved ones and the time with friends that can give you a sense of, "Yeah I can make it" but the choice is totally up to you. I heard a lot from my in-laws that I was a "strong woman and a smart girl" and that I knew but I did not know how to put that in action. Let me be real for a minute, yes, I was strong and smart, but one thing that I had to get together once again was patience and letting God be God. During this time of waiting, I still pressed on even when I did not feel like it because I wanted to go through this thing ONCE! I listened to spiritual counsel, grabbed myself by the bootstraps and prepared not only my natural case, but yielding to His will at the same time.

I was in the process of a divorce, being evicted from the family home that we rented and possibly losing my means of transportation. I had more bills than money and I could not handle all that was coming in with the finances from the salon as well as maintaining everything else. Yes, I was getting financial help from my husband, but not much, not at around the same time of the month and not enough to help keep everything going in the home. I felt that nothing in my life was consistent, or at least that was what I thought. God was consistent every step of the way and when I think about it, He was there the whole time. Every month all the bills were paid, even at the salon. My landlords at both the house and salon were so understanding and extremely helpful. They made sure that they did whatever it took to make sure that myself and my girls were ok.

I remember it like yesterday, I had been dealing with a lot and the bills were coming due. I got up and went to church and for some reason the parking lot was full on the side I normally park on, and I had to park on the side near the multipurpose building. It was just me and my oldest girl because the younger two were off visiting their father. After service was over, I talked to a few people and headed to the car. I had already made my petitions know unto the Lord about what I needed and what was needed to be done in the house. As I was walking down the hall to the exit door, I was stopped by one of the ladies that I had worked with years prior in the church office. She stopped me and informed me of a bet that we had made as I was training her to take over my Administrative duties. I had no idea of what the bet was, and I had forgotten about it, because it was so long ago, and we were just joking. She advised me that she owed me and wanted to settle the debt. I told her that it did not matter because I did not remember and If I lost, I did not have the money to pay her. We laughed and she said, "No! God has been too good to me and I am going to keep my word." I finally agreed to the payment and assumed that it was just a few dollars. She comes back with a check and said that she did not have time to get cash, but the check is good and if I had any issues cashing it let her know. Guys, the check was in the amount of $500!! I told her I could not accept that amount and that it was too much. She insisted and we hugged, and I cried. It was enough to pay my car note and a few other things I needed to purchase. I cried all the way home, and I knew then that God was working on my behalf and I was going to be alright.

This was one of the many of things that God was doing to ensure that I had everything that I needed to get through this horrible time in my life. My aunt and cousin came together to make sure that I had a lawyer, a few more family members gave to me and the girls. One of my aunts used her points through her timeshare to take us on vacation to get our minds off all that we were going through. My village as I call them, came by, and called all the time and offered whatever they could. One of the greatest things that you can have when going through any type of season in your life, are true friends and family that will stick by you through the good and bad as well as pray with and for you. I love my village!

I was on my way to pick up the girls from school, I parked in the teachers parking lot because I arrived early. I began to talk to God, and it was the most honest thing that I could have ever said to Him. "God I'm scared!" When it was time, I entered the cafeteria and waited for the girls to enter the afterschool program. While I was waiting, I heard it so clearly, "Pray through your fear". Those 4 words gave me so much peace and confidence and to this day, anytime I feel scared, I pray through it. The following week I had had a conversation with my landlord about the house and what was to take place next. I called my attorney's office and while waiting on a returned phone call, I was driving up the road talking to God. I am a weeper so of course the tears were falling, but my prayer was different this time. It was, "Lord if You don't do it, It Won't get done!" I meant that thing with everything in me because I had no way to make a move with little finances.

When the lady at my attorney's office called me back, she asked me what was going on. I explained to her that the rent had not been paid and that we were going to be evicted. Now this is the same lady that was so rude to me when I was trying to first get in an appointment with the attorney. She stated that she wanted to talk to me personally, because she too was experiencing something in her marriage, and she was facing the same thing. She told me what she had been going through in her marriage of over 20 years and we began to weep together. She encouraged me so and assured me that everything was gonna be alright and she would make sure that whatever I needed to keep me and my girls in that home, she was gonna do it. This was a complete turnaround from someone who was so rude to me, to helping me fight for what I needed. God will use any and every individual to work on your behalf, even when you have no idea.

I went on about my day and I had decided to hang out with some of the ladies for movie and dinner. I had a gift card from Christmas that I never used for the movies and once I got to the restaurant, I ran into Terry and her husband, whom I call my big brother and sister. As they were leaving from having their dinner, Terry came over and slipped me some money and told me that dinner was on them. The next day, I was out buying some much-needed sneakers for the girls, so I placed them on my Belk card to prevent the use of cash. As we were trying to decide what shoes to buy, my phone rang. The person on the other end asked how I was doing and after talking for a few, she stated that she had something for me and that it was laid on her heart to do it. She asked where I was, and she came and met me at the mall. I had no idea what it was but thank you Lord for whatever it was. She handed me an envelope and said that she could not sleep, because she heard about my situation, and she talked it over with her husband and they wanted to be a blessing to me and my girls. I told her thank you and that I was grateful for whatever it was, and we parted ways. I opened the envelope and there were 10 $100 bills! I pulled over and screamed, the girls were in the back seat of the car asking what was wrong, because I scared them. I told them what had happened and spoke with them about how doing things right and paying your tithes will open doors. I nervously drove up the street to my mom's job and told her what had happened, and she started running and praising God right there in her store. As I left and head home, I called my landlord and reminded him of the words that I spoke to him and God. I said, "Remember I told you that if God didn't do it, it won't get done!" He said he remembered, and I told him that I needed to send him the rent money and he was in such disbelief. He stated that my faith reminded me of his mother and that is one of the reasons he and his wife felt compelled to work with me through this ordeal. They lowered my rent down to $800, because they wanted to make sure that the girls finish school and not be interrupted with a move. They also wanted to give me time to see what was going to happen with my finances in order to stay in the house. They were going to sign a new lease with me at a lower rate on the original lease, because of everything that I was going through. He reassured me that when it came down to it, they were "Team Meko" and would do all he and his wife could for me. The sad part is that I never had the chance to sign the new lease because it was taking forever to get to court to figure out the finances.

By this time, I was attending my church during the 11am service, go home and feed the girls, and then headed to the church I am now a member of at 3pm. This was the same church that I had attended for the Ordination of my friend. It started with me attending Bible study for a series on Spiritual Warfare. I did the two services for months and I finally decided that The Birthing Worship Cathedral was where I wanted to be. I loved the teachings, which was so in-depth, and I learned so much in Bible study and the 3pm services were like nothing I had seen in years. After some time of truly debating, I decided to move my membership to the Birthing Worship Cathedral. I completed all of my assignments and tasks at my former church with excellence and I later turned in my letter of resignation. This was one of the hardest decisions that I had to make, because I had been a part of this Ministry for well over 13 years.

While you are waiting, God is working! My daughter's friends who call me Ma, made sure that whatever car repairs that I needed; they took care of it. I had money coming in from the north, south, east, and west at one point. When it was time for me to finally leave the rental home, I was at ease and I was at peace. It was time for me to leave because the finances were getting tight and while he was living the good life, we were losing our home. I packed up the house and place my things in storage and moved in with my cousin. Me and the little ones shared a room and my oldest slept in another room/office. This was not the easiest thing for me to do, because I was used to being on my own and having my own space. I truly thank God that she had the room to place us in, but even in that situation it was moments of grief, feeling defeated, unhappiness and my sense of comfort was no more. My plan was to stay for a few months and find a place in the area, but that was not God's plan, I stayed six months. I had to sit and learn one of the biggest lessons I had neglected to learn the first time. After my prayer time, I sat at the kitchen table and I heard it so clear, "I placed you hear to teach you to be quiet!"

Think back to when He sent word for me to stop arguing and just be quiet. Now, the human side wants the last word or the petty response, but this particular day I heard it loud and clear. There was an incident that took place with my youngest daughter and another little girl that she would hang with at her father's house. I had no idea as to what had taken place between the two girls and I had been thrown into the mix without knowing all the details. When my phone rang, I was still unaware as to what was going on. He asked me what it was that I said to the little girl and he proceeded to get loud, so I hung up the phone. My phone rang again, and I answered in my nice petty voice and the attitude was still there… Now, I'm getting upset and letting him know that I would not be spoken to like that and also, I informed him that I did not know too much about the situation. Little did I know that I was on speaker phone and there was more than one person on the call. Well… Ms. Ma'am decided to chime in and by then I had put it together that he need to show her that he could handle me… Sooo, I had the attitude like, "Oh You Wanna Talk To Meee!!" Once again, I felt myself leave my body as I spoke some words that I had not spoken in an awfully long time. By the time I was done, I was ready to pop the trunk! Nobody was coming or said they were, but dang it, I was ready, because I was tired of being pushed. To this day some of my friends say I am too Christian(y), because I would always say and believe that in due time God would handle it. We laugh about it now, but trust I was going to lay hands that day. As long as I had my tire iron, that is all I needed. Now I am not proud of this but when I think about that day, I was crazy and ready to take my mug shot with a smile. Lord Help! I called my Bishop and asked him where he was, because I was about to go to jail. I am laughing so hard as I type this, because I am giving you all the honest truth about this moment to make a point.

He told me that, he had been to the doctor with his son and could not answer my first call. I explained what happened and, in my mind, they were coming, and I was about to handle business. He was asking if he needed to come and see what was going on, but as I spoke, he listened. After I was done, he stopped for a second and asked if I was completely finished. Now when Bishop Smith starts any conversation off with, "Now Daughter" you already know you are about to be told something that is going to get you right together or calm you down. In this instance he did both. Bishop gave me some wise instructions and told me how it worked for him in a situation he was faced with and I promise you, that once I grasp hold to that wisdom, (finally) that is when I started to see the change in me and what I was once allowing to take my peace was no more. See, you have to get to a place where your peace of mind is better than anything in the world and you will not allow anything to disrupt it.

Chapter 7

FALSE LABOR

June 16, 2018

Last night, well this morning I had another dream. I dreamt that I was pregnant and I began spotting. It was not like the last dream I had some time ago where the blood was flowing, in this dream I was spotting, but still cause for concern. The lady that was treating me was not my regular doctor, I had never seen her before; she was beautiful and had these long black dreads. It was crazy in the beginning because I was there at the hospital already to be of support to someone else. I ended up on the table in the ER and they were going to take the baby, but they found that I had a slight fever and that would not go well with the meds that they were going to give me, so they called it off and was sending me home to rest. I was frustrated because the doctor left and did not admit me to watch for infection, she just said go home and rest. I could not understand why she would just send me home with my previous pregnancy medical history. Before I knew it, she had on all white and some fabulous white heels and she walked away, or shall I say she disappeared.

When I awoke, I immediately wrote the dream in my book. I was telling my aunt Jerrilene about it and she told me that it may mean that "What I was carrying, it was not time for me to give birth to it as of yet. If the doctor would have taken the baby prematurely it would have possibly died. I was sent home to rest and not stress, because it was not time to give "birth" to this baby yet. I had to allow God to finish the process." To me it made sense, because there were times in my waiting that I wanted to give up and just be done with the whole thing. There were also times when the blows and attacks were so much that I thought I was going to lose it. In the midst of it all, I knew that when it got to be too much for me to handle, I would remember my Yes, and keep pushing. I look back at it now and I think to myself that if I had just listened and did what God had instructed in the beginning, I would not have had to go through as much as I did. Even with that thought, I still believe that going left instead of going right, taught me some of my greatest lessons that I needed to learn. No, you will not always get every move or thing right, but it is what you take from it that matters. I learned the meaning of silence, I learned humility, I gained confidence in who I was and whose I was, and I also learned submission.

What I mean by learning submission is that I had to do a little more surrendering to God than normal. I had to be uncomfortable in a season of brokenness and rebuilding. No one likes the tearing down, the ripping, and or the breaking. You may experience one of these things or you may experience all three. Well, I had all three, but the best part about it was, I was ready to surrender on my own, because I was just that tired. I did not want God to make me surrender unto Him, I wanted to do it on my own, so if another situation arises, I will intuitively know how to surrender it to God and let it go. It was not comfortable living in one room with my two little ones, going from a climbing credit score to bad credit, bill collectors calling and wondering what was next to come. I had to continue to wait until God was done doing what He needed to get me to a place, that I believe that I could hear Him with clarity and move when He said move. Thanksgiving and Christmas came and went and before you knew it another year was here. I was still waiting and going through some changes in the house that we were stay in and all the while still walking in love and trying to be the best I can. See there is nothing like going through something, being uncomfortable and having you kids ask you over and over, "When are we moving Mom?" I heard that almost every week the last few months of living there. Now that kind of pressure is enough to make you scream. One thing for sure, our kids look for us as parents to make things happen and they do not understand the process of a thing. There were long waiting lists for apartments in the area that I was living in at the time, because it was a small town, and a lot of people was relocating to that particular area. I called everywhere, drove around looking for places and I even tried Habitat for Humanity, and I was denied twice. The pressure was unreal, but even in it I was still grateful for the roof over our heads.

January 3, 2019, the scariest day in my life was finally here! I had to do something that I had never done in my life, take the stand in court. We had been to court once prior to in June the previous year, but that was due to error on his part and some other business that needed to be handled. I was overly prepared for court and I had all that I needed and then some. See, let me take a minute and show you how God watches out for His children. Sometimes when people are trying to get out of a thing that they do not take the time to close doors, but when you lived your whole life of leaving doors open, you don't think about it. You never, ever rush to get out of a thing, but if you must leave do it the right way and then move on. I had so much information and things at my access, that it would blow your mind if I told you how I got it; yes, it was legal. It was wide open for me to have and all I had to do was walk through the door. Even by me being still and sitting back, information of all avenues was coming to me from all sorts of ways and I did not have to ask for it. I knew so much that it would have made their heads spin. I pretty much knew every detail of their lives without having to fish for it. All that hell that I had been put through was for a reason and in the end, it worked to my advantage. Let me tell you something, When I was out of pocket with God, I was dealt with by Him but when you sow, trust, and believe, God always keeps His promises. Okay now back to the court proceedings, I was calm and answered every question that my lawyer asked and believe me he was very thorough. I brought a lot of information to light and upon the time I was supposed to be cross examined, his lawyer declined to do so. One thing is for certain and two things are for sure, these judges are not new to the schemes and shenanigans of the person in the wrong. I am going to just leave that right there. I was awarded in my efforts and I left the court with a little more peace.

After being told that it would be difficult to get approved for an apartment, because of the eviction on my record, I had no idea how this was going to work. I got up one morning and I was sitting on the side of the bed and this one complex came to me back in the city of Savannah. I called them and the lady was so excited, and they had all kinds of move in specials and fees waived. I drove down and spoke to the lady and once she heard about my eviction, she told me that I would not be approved. Now if I would have gotten up out of that seat only God knows where I would have been. She asked what I did for a living and I told her that I owned my own salon and it turned into another 30-minute conversation about her hair. I explained my situation and did a little name drop of who my Bishop was to the manager and she immediately knew who I was speaking of. The lady at the front desk just told me to go ahead and fill out the application and get it back to her. A few days later I received a call letting me know that I was approved, but I was first denied. They denied me, but she said that it was something about me and she sent it up the latter and they gave the go ahead. Within two weeks we had deposits, rent and utilities paid and was move in ready. I made sure that when I left my current situation, I left it nice and clean and on a good note. Do not tell me what God cannot do! Prior to the move, sometime in

December I was in service. My Bishop looked over to me after he finished preaching. He spoke into the microphone, "Tamiko Gregory, you will receive a call withing the next few weeks from your husband, asking to meet with you to ask you what it is that you want." He was speaking of a financial resolution in the divorce. I made a face, because I did not want to meet with him and then I heard, "fix your face, everything you want, you're gonna get it." He also said, "I see a white woman giving you the keys to your own place within 30 days and she's gonna tell you to stay as long as you want." I had never been so happy to hear those words. By the way, I received a text almost 3 weeks later asking me what it is that I wanted, and he and his attorney were going to try to come up with a solution. I did listen, but I did not trust it too much, especially not having my attorney in on it. While I'm Waiting!

Chapter 8

THE LIE

Going back to the first book of Samuel and around chapter 19, you read how Saul took David into his home. Saul's son Jonathan immediately knitted to the soul of David and he loved David as his very own brother. They made a covenant and Jonathan took off his own robe and gave it to David along with his armor, sword, bow and his belt. David went wherever Saul had sent him and he behaved wisely, because he was fully submitted to Saul and served him wisely in every way that he could. David understood where his blessing came from and we have to have that same spirit of doing things wisely and not go low when others do. Saul became angry because David was, in my words, accepted and admired by the people of Israel as well as Saul's servants. Although he received all this praise, he still remained humbled and continued to serve Saul wisely.

Being that Saul was not impressed by the idea of David getting more praise from the people of Israel, he became angry with David to the point of trying and wanting to kill him. Now I brought this back up because, it was in this reading again that I realized that out of all the things Saul did to David and David was aware of it, but he still chose to handle things the right way. He knew where his blessings came from and he respected the office of Saul and the love that he had for Jonathan. So, I had to grasp that thing and understand that no matter what happens, still treat them with love and kindness, treat the situation wisely and most importantly pray for them. I was given some great advice a long time ago from my former First Lady, she said, "Sometimes you just have to pray for people, at first you're not gonna want to really pray for them, but the more that you do, it will get easier and easier and one day you're going to mean it and pray for them with sincerity." I still believe that to this day because it really does happen that way.

There is nothing like having a piece of mind and having a deeper understanding of what you went through and why. Although things are getting better for me and my girls, I on the other hand, am still not done, Waiting! While I am waiting, I am still on this emotional rollercoaster. They come in waves and the anxiety is still rearing its head at times. Yes, I am more confident, but I am now the head of my household, running a business, maintaining my girl's wellbeing, and dealing with the spirit of loneliness. Even in conversations you know in the back of your mind that you are still married, but the attention is so refreshing. Then there is the Spiritual fight and the wanting to do all that you can to go through this thing the right way and all you want to do is be pleasing in the Lord's sight. I would always say that I came too far to mess up now. Trust me it has not always been easy, and you make a lot of mistakes, but one thing that I had to learn was to be confident in my own skin. Love me and appreciate every curve, flaw, stretch mark and everything else that makes me who I am.

Trying to be the head of the house and making sure that everything runs smoothly was sometimes a lot of weight on my shoulder. I had forgotten at times who my source was, and I had to remember to move me out of the way and let God be God. I sat down with my Bishop and we went over my intake of income from the business and court appointed income. We reviewed every single bill that I had and how to manage and budget my finances, we would come and review within six months to see how far I had come. There were many conversations in between due to the frustration of all that was going on. One night I was working late, and I had not gotten home until 10pm and I only had my youngest with me at the time. There were no parking spaces left and I had to back up and go all the way to the front of the complex and walk through the path. I saw a tow truck doing a U-turn and because I was so tired, I thought no more about it. Little did I know that they were looking for my vehicle. I went in the house and I told my daughter that once she returned home that she would have to park where I was. She notified me that she had not seen my car but parked there anyway. I still had not put two and two together, because I was so exhausted from working all day.

We got up the next morning and we all left the house at the same time, I was heading to the salon and my daughter was going to her place of employment. My car was gone!! It all came back to me that the tow truck was there for my car. It was hard playing catch up and because I was not in charge of paying my car note the few years prior, I had no more deferments left and by the time the car note was turned over to me I was almost 3 months behind. Not one tear was shed for the loss of the car, I believe that I was in shock more than anything. I had forgot to call them back to make a payment, it totally slipped my mind. Yes, it was easier said than done to go get another job and work the salon and make sure the kids were secured, but it was not that simple. They were out of school and who was going to keep them? I have a room in the salon that they use to hang out in while I work. I know, I know the mom sometimes has to carry the load, but I was always taught that we have to do what we must to make it work. For the first time in almost a year and a half I could breathe. I was not sad to have lost my vehicle, I was actually relieved. My daughter offered me her car to have and she would still pay the note. I told her that would not be necessary, she needed her vehicle.

Not even a week later, I received a call asking me how I was doing. She said that she was not trying to get in my business, but she had heard that I lost my car. I told her I did, and she asked did I want it back, and I told her I did not. I could not afford to keep that car and then the insurance was a lot too. She asked how I felt, and I told her that I was finally able to breathe and she said, "Good, breathe!" She told me that there was a car that was sent to her and for me to call and see if the car were still available and then see if my uncle could go with me to look at it. She sent me the pictures and the information, and I went and looked at the car the next day. We did the test drive, and I loved the fact that it was a Camry and had a sunroof. My uncle did a good look over and said that it was a good car. They did some work to it and they put new tires on it. I made an offer lower than what they wanted, and I reassured them that I would be there the next day to purchase it. I called her back and told her what my uncle said, and she asked did I want it and I did. Needless to say, I picked the car up the next day, paid in full!

Even after all of that I was still feeling some kind of way.

May 28, 2019

No one can tell me how I'm feeling right now. This emotional rollercoaster is a little much. I have lost a husband, a home, a car, and all that I had known to be normal. Over the course of it all I have grown and learned my strength. There are times when I don't want to be strong, I just want things to be how they used to be, but I know that all of this that I'm going through is for the sacrifice and the Glory of God. But one thing for sure, I have to take my eyes off my situation and the natural and see what God is doing and what He is saying.

I'm still hearing the sounds of II Samuel 1:15 coming back to me these last few days and I am not sure as to what more that God is saying to me concerning this passage of scripture. I did some praying on it and I believe that I got some clarity on it a little better, so now all I have to do it wait until it plays out.

I received a call from my attorney's office letting me know that we have a court date set for the final hearing and after this date my divorce would be over. The reality was setting in, but this time I was in a better place. All I wanted was for this thing to be over and I can finally move on with my life. Not so much in the dating world, but my freedom and my new life can begin. After the call they sent an email with all the information attached to it and we set up a date to come together and prepare for my case. After some time, I took the time to reflect and think about all that I had been through and all the mess that caused havoc in the life of myself and the life of my girls. I looked back from the very beginning of this thing and how far I had come. I remembered back in December of 2018, at 2:55pm I remember writing, "and just in this moment, I feel free!! I feel a heaviness that has been lifted, like I was carrying a heavy weight. I feel so empty and I feel like I want to cry from the emotions of feeling free."

While I was preparing for court and trying to get all my affairs in order, my daughter had to go to training in Atlanta, Ga. Since the girls would be away visiting their father, I decided to tag along with her. We got to Atlanta and got checked in, went to dinner, and ended the evening at Walmart to pick up snacks for the room. She gave me the bed and she took the pull out. It felt so good to get away, it is something about being out of Chatham County that makes you feel better. I took my laptop and all the paperwork that I needed to continue to prepare for court. While my daughter was away at training the next morning, I stayed at the hotel and continued to work and register for a Parenting Transitional class that is required when going through divorce with children. Thank God that I did not wait, because there was one class that was left to take before my court date. My daughters' training class let out early and we headed downtown, to hang out and we ended up going to the Coca Cola Factory. We had so much fun walking downtown and through the park. The tour of the factory was remarkably interesting, and we had the opportunity to taste Coke from all over the world. Some of the different flavors were good and there were some that were absolutely horrible. Of course, the trip could not be complete without dinner at the Cheesecake Factory. It is our favorite place to eat, well for me I like P.F. Changs, but nobody that I travel with wants to go eat there, but you can best believe before I left to head home, I was going to go get my shrimp and lobster fried rice. We headed back to the hotel, because we had had a long day of fun and Brittney had to get up for training in the morning. On the last day of our visit, I was able to get a late check out, so I took Brittney to training and came back to the hotel. I got ready and packed up my things. I decided that I was going to the movies while she was in class, but the movie did not start until 1pm. Brittney called and asked if I could give her and a few of her friends a lift to the mall for lunch. That was perfect because I could eat lunch with her and do a little looking around until the movie starts. I dropped them back off to training and I headed to the movie theatre to see a movie called *Ma*. I have never ever been to the movies by myself, so this was a big deal for me. I got my ticket and headed in; I was the only one in there until a few others walked in. I was the only one in there until a few others walked in. The theatre was already dark when I entered so I sat behind a half wall partition. How about all the previews were of upcoming horror movies. Really? I was a big girl, and the movie was awesome! I did a little bit of sightseeing and the headed to the training site because I knew that they would be out soon. Once she was done, I went to P.F. to get my rice and we also got cheesecake to go. The ride home was a good one, it felt so good to get away.

You know, God will never leave you out of the loop. I received a call from my Bishop letting me know what God had given him concerning me and my upcoming court case, so I made sure that I had all that particular information ready and every single I was dotted. I took the Transitional Parenting class, I believe on a Saturday morning and I will tell you, that this class is something that I believe everyone should take. It was so informative and I wish that I would have taken this class much earlier and I wished that because my husband had taken it early on, that he would have put a lot of that information to use. I met with my attorney to prep for court and go over some documents that were sent over from my husband's attorney. I went over that paperwork with a fine-tooth comb and made a list of questions. We spent 2 hours preparing for court and I was ready and prepared for what was to come. Now by this time, I am in a whole new mindset and I have a new way of thinking and feeling. This was almost over, and I can finally move on with my life.

Date: Unknown (2018), Dream

I was sitting at the table with my attorney in the court room waiting on the decision of the judge. I was so nervous, because never in my life had I ever been through such an ordeal and I have never been divorced before. The judge walked in and after we sat back down, I grabbed my attorneys' hand. I was so scared as to what was to happen next. My leg was shaking, and my palms were sweaty. I was thinking to myself; Did I do this all for nothing and will I walk away in tears? She gave her verdict and stated all the things that I would be getting in the divorce. I began to squeeze the hand of my attorney and the tears began to flow. I came out with more than I expected, and I just sat there in disbelief.

I am not sure exactly when this dream took place, but I knew it was at a time when I was still fighting for my marriage and I did not want it to end. Although he was gone, I was still willing to do whatever I needed to, to make us work and to put my family back together. So, when I had this dream, I was not receiving it at all and that, I believe this started my mixed feelings and my emotional rollercoaster trying my hardest to accept that my marriage was possibly dissolving. God give me understanding because I am still waiting!

Chapter 9

IT WAS GOOD THAT I WAS AFFLICTED

While I sat at my dining room table, studying the book of Corinthians, I was reading about forgiveness. I feel that I have grown so much during this time in my life and that there were things that I would have never saw myself accepting years prior. In the second chapter and the tenth verse it says, *"To whom ye forgive anything, I forgive also: for if I forgave anything, to whom I forgave it, for your sakes forgave I it in the person of Christ."* In this instance Paul shows real compassion and wisdom when he tells the Corinthians to forgive and comfort the man. The man that Paul was speaking of did wrong and he had to be punished, but once he repented for his wrongdoing, he was comforted by them and forgiven.

Not everyone who has wronged you will come to you and apologize or come with a repented heart to fix what they may have done to you. It is up to you to forgive them, even if the apology or a mend never takes place. One thing is for certain and two things are for sure, that if you have truly forgiven someone, you will notice the change in YOU! This change will allow you to accept the forgiveness in such a loving manner and even if the apology never happens, you will be at peace with it anyway. See Paul instructs us to forgive and comfort, because although the offense may make it harder to forgive and it leaves you aware of what happened in the past, comfort takes it to heart and the heart forgives. This is how we expect God to forgive us, so we must learn to do the same with others. Have you ever thought about it like this? The one who caused the offense may be so bound with guilt of what they have done, that they themselves feel bad or is so prideful that they just do not know how to say I am sorry. I have learned to look at it from a different point of view and not a view of my own wanting. Sometimes we want something so bad to satisfy our flesh, until we do not allow God to do what He needs to do in us. I imagined on so many occasions of an apology being given to me, but I had to get a place of moving on without one, because I may never get one. As I said before, I was no angel, and I may have a few apologies of my own to give.

The day has finally arrived! The girls are with their father for the week and so I am able to get up and get myself together. I was a nervous wreck, and I was all over the place. I had to be to the courthouse by 9am and I was up in enough time to try on about 3 different outfits. I will never forget the date; Monday, July 1, 2019. I was making good time, I wanted to get there early because of parking in the garage would fill quickly. Upon arriving, I get a text from my husband wanting to know about meeting with him and our attorneys for one final try to come up with an agreement prior to court. Of course, that did not happen and the fact that his lawyer was so loud with his game plan was not a help to them at all. Not much after sitting down with my lawyer and going over some papers, we were told that we had to come back at 2pm due to some delay. This was nerve racking because my day was drawn out a little bit longer. I was sent on a mission from my lawyer to find some paperwork that was needed. I went home and pulled it up on the computer and once I found it, I printed it out and made it back downtown to attend the 2pm session and of course all the parking spaces were taken. Time was winding down and I was getting frustrated. I finally found a place to park, and I made it in maybe a few minutes prior to court. I calmed myself down, strapped my shoe and calmly walked into the courtroom. After getting settled in the courtroom, all the cases had been introduced, and of course we were up first. I took the stand, I believe, and I was able to answer all the question that was asked by my attorney and then some. He took his time and brought a lot of information to light and even the judge had a few questions for me as well. Upon cross examination, I found that they had little to go off of and they really were not as prepared as I thought. When it was my husband's turn to take the stand, his lawyer questioned him for a few minutes and then it was our time for cross examination. I must say, that although I did not understand the process of my attorneys' office outside of the courtroom, he was absolutely brilliant and thorough. He took his time questioning my soon to be ex-husband for a great deal of time. After all was said and done and all closing arguments were made…. It was time to hear what the judge had to say and then this would all be over. My palms were sweaty, and my heart was beating out of my chest. I think I was a little more nervous, because an old classmate of mine was there going through the same thing and all my business was on front street.

The judge took a few minutes to write a few things down and crunch some numbers, at this point I'm even more panicked, because I don't know what is about to come out of her mouth. She said, "The systems are down!!" Unbeknownst to us the Child Support calculator was down, and we could not resolve that particular matter and she wanted to make sure that I would be getting the correct amount. After the judge explained how the calculator worked and how she would like to wait for it to come back up, the words that came from her mouth next reminded me of the dream that I had some time prior. See when I dream, I have to write it down, because I need to be absolutely sure that it is not just me and it is God. Everything that we asked for and then some was given to me. I could not believe what was happening at that moment, it was like I was living my dream all over again. I left feeling like David who had just defeated Goliath! All the things, hurt, anger, pain, plots, tricks, and schemes that took place over the years had paid off. I never understood where all the nastiness and such anger would come from someone that I had loved for well over 15 years. Never in my wildest dreams did I ever see this man treating me as such, let alone allowing someone else to join in to add pain in my life. One thing about God is that His word does not lie. He said that He would bottle every tear and every battle belongs to Him. I walked out of that courtroom feeling like a 300lb weight had been lifted off of my shoulders. The judge still had some considerations to consider, but it was all in my favor. As I walked back to the car, I could not contain my excitement, but at the same time I felt sorry for him, only because I already knew what was coming. I made a few calls on the ride home and once I got home, I undressed and laid in my bed. All I could do was thank God and cry in the amazement of Him. I was so thankful and grateful that after all of this, it was finally over! Well so I thought….

For over a month the systems were down, and I was once again sitting on the edge of my seat wondering when I will be free from this marriage. It was not until sometime in October that I was informed that I was finally divorced. I had a detail description of all of the things that I was granted in the divorce and when I say I got it all, I got it all and the overall rights of the two little ones. Now let me back up to the month of August and all that happened. The girls are gone for a visit with their father and they mentioned a wedding. I was totally confused because I did not know you could remarry prior to divorce. It was on a Sunday when I started receiving pictures and videos of a wedding ceremony. It is funny because all I could see was my freedom and the fact that I was not responsible for his covering anymore and our legal covenant was no more. We got up to sing for Praise and Worship and we began to sing a song called *Freedom*. When we got to the part of singing *no more shackles, no more chains, no more bondage, I am free...yeah.* I was singing to my future, but I was still curious as to how a ceremony could take place and we are still married. Well, he must have gotten his copy of the decree prior to me receiving mine and come to find out I had been divorced since July 1st. I just did not receive my decree until October and my ex-husband received his a few days prior to getting remarried in August, I assume.

Chapter 10

WHILE I'M WAITING

I was officially free from all that I had known over the last 17 and a half years and I was alright with that. I was in a place of peace and in a place in my life where I was excited to see what my future had in store. God said that He knew the thoughts that He thought towards me, thoughts of peace, and not of evil, to give me an expected end. He also said in His word that He would turn me away from my captivity and will gather me from all the nations and all the places whither He have driven me and He will bring me again into the place where He once caused me to be carried away captive. I remember not long after everything happened, I was talking with a friend of mine. We had several conversations and there was this one question that she had asked me that made me think, but my answer was so profound and clear. She asked, "What is your fear in all of this?" I replied, "That I would outgrow him!" I have done just that during my time of healing and moving forward. Again, I will say this this has not been easy, but now looking back at it all, I am grateful for so many reasons. The first thing is that I was chosen to go through this ordeal and that God had that much faith in my ability to stand. That in the times where I thought I was going to lose my mind and fall apart, I had so many people praying for me, encouraging me and cheering me on. That I made it through it all with my dignity and that me and my girls are stronger and closer than ever. I am moving forward in Ministry, making great strides in my life and I can say without a shadow of a doubt, that I did it the right way!

Once I finally gathered myself and allowed my focus to shift, that is when I started noticing more that God was digging in more to those that played a part in my marriage. I know that I wanted to handle them myself, but I had to remember that God's timing for them was a thing too. When you see and hear of the "vengeance" that was released on those that hurt you, it doesn't make you feel like celebrating. What I mean by that is that God can take care of people better than we can and there are no limits to His reach. You will find that your heart has changed towards the situation when you begin to hear all that is and has happened to them. Over time my prayers for them, went from do whatever you see fit to Lord have mercy upon them. Why? Because I had forgiven them, and I had forgiven them whole heartedly. I never knew how God was gonna do it, but just that He would, and I was so amazed that I began to pray for them instead of celebrating that it finally happened. Things were happening all along, but the bigger things took place a later on, once I got quiet and let it all go. Everything that God had given me concerning him, had come to past with the exception of a few things. It wasn't revealed to me anything about her until this one

Sunday the guest speaker reminded me that God had not forgotten about her. From my knowledge this lady had no idea what was going on in my life to know that there was another woman involved in my marriage.

I often wonder why God chose or allowed me to go through this. I also wonder what it would have been like for me, if I had been the one to walk away? I look back at some of my memories in old journals and memories on social media and there were many times that I wanted to leave. I think the thing for me was, not that it was over, but how it happened. I know that I spoke of this before, but that reality just sunk in a little deeper. I feel that I have more than I have had in an awfully long time. No, I'm not talking about the material things, I grew tired of the material things a long time ago. I'm speaking of the peace in my life, the freedom to choose and not settling, my ambition, my motivation and most importantly finding my true self. I had to fall in love with me in my time of waiting, fall in love with being me outside of being a wife, a mother, and a Minister. I found that I am so much more and there is more in my future. As of now I live in a 2-bedroom apartment and driving an older model Camry that is paid for and I am just as content as I have been in years. I have the love of my babies, my family, and the people that are in my circle that loves me unconditionally.

And I will restore to you the years that the locust hath eaten, the cankerworm, and the caterpillar, and the palmerworm, my great army which I sent among you.

I always remember my former Pastor and mentor, she used to always say that God was "The Redeemer of Time" and this kept ringing with me. Even in those dark moments, I always looked forward to the future, even when I could not see one. God promised me that He was gonna not only restore me, but the things that I lost due to all that I had endured. I was having a conversation one day with Bishop Smith and he asked me something that I had not thought about or questioned in an awfully long time. He asked me if God had ordained for me and my ex-husband to marry? I paused and thought about it, but I could not fully answer, well at least I thought that we were meant to be together forever. He went on to explain that although it may or may not have been God's will for the marriage or anything that we do in life, but God gives us grace in it and grace to get through it.

I had gotten through the hardest time in my life and I was finally starting to see stability. Even after my court win, I was still having doubts about having to carry a full household on my own as well as a business. I had to come to the realization that my greater was coming and God was going to continue to sustain that business and help me with carrying the house. Well, God did just that, there was already one young lady renting a chair and a few months later I had another renter. With the three of us working together, it has gotten to the place where the salon maintained itself. I never not once had a struggle of paying bills for both the business and home. I take no credit for none of this, I give God all the praise for sustaining me when I had no idea how I was gonna make it. Even when I made very little at the salon, I tithed off of it. There were times my tithes were only $12 and there were times my tithes were more than I could have imagined in a week's time, but I was always faithful. I even tithed off of all the monies that were given to me to help pay bills. I honestly believe that that too is where my increase comes from. We never went without food or anything that we needed for our everyday needs. My prayer was and will always be that I be a good steward over my finances and just because I have it does not mean that I need to spend it.

I was so looking forward to the year 2020, because it was going to be the year of perfect vision. I along with everybody else was looking forward to this New Year beginning and then here comes COVID-19. I had no idea what was going to happen to us and how we were going to sustain to keep going in such a crisis. I was instructed to close the salon for the month of April, and I was closed for half of the month of May. I cannot tell you how we sustained and how we still never went without. All of the bills at the house and the salon was paid every single month. I saved more than half of my taxes and the stimulus check that was given from the government because I was doing so well. Never once was I worried about how things were going to get done, because I had learned during my season of stretching that God was my ultimate source. I had always depended on my ex-husband to carry everything, but I had to learn that he wasn't even the source of us having what we had, it was all God! He did more than I ever expected!

Just because I came through this does not mean that my waiting period is over, it just shifted to another area of my life. I am waiting to see where God is taking me in this next season of my life. I believe that waiting is something that we all must do in every aspect of our lives; the key is HOW WE ARE WAITING! Are you waiting in fear? Are you waiting with expectation? Are you waiting or wasting time? How are you WAITING? *While I'm Waiting*, is not just a statement, it's an ACTION! Waiting means to stay where one is or delaying action until a particular time or until something else happens. Are you willing to wait until something happens? Now before you answer that question, you have to understand that not everything happens right away. It takes patience and a whole lot of trust. Trusting God in the process. Remember I spoke about that in the beginning of the book. I remember I was telling God that I didn't want to go through this for a long period of time and I just knew God was gonna just step in and make it all right in a few months. Child-please I went through this thing for almost 2 years. Tell God what you don't want and watch what happens. I may have even been a part of the delay process by not being obedient and following instructions, there were times I went left when He pointed, revealed, and even confirmed me to go right.

I wouldn't change what I have been through because it has made and molded me into the person I am today.

I never thought that all my pain was a set up for my greatest victory. I cannot believe where I am and all that I have accomplished. I can honestly say with every fiber of my being, I AM GLAD THAT I WAS AFFLICTED!! This journey has taught me so much about who I am and how incredibly strong that I am. I cannot wait to see all that is in store for me and my babies in the future. I can admit that I still have a little residue from my first marriage, but I expect that I will be totally healed, and residue free before HE sends me the man that He has designed just for me. Oh yeah, I will do it again, but in His timing……. I'm Still Waiting!!

The purpose behind your pain is that there is a product that God is trying to produce. It is necessary in order for God to get the Glory. The pain will leave when it is finished teaching you!

- *John Gray*

October 5, 2020

I sat at the dining room table and opened my laptop. After checking my email, bank account, and of course my Facebook account I made my morning coffee and breakfast. I'm not sure what made me do it, but I opened Microsoft Word and began typing my first line… "What the Hell". The year before at my birthday dinner, I was laughing with some friends of mine about my book title. As I began to type I realized that I was gonna need my journal to get the proper information in order to do this. I had gotten two chapters in and I found that I was getting angry all over again. Why was I getting angry when all I wanted to do was tell my story because I thought I was in a place of, "I'm fine" I was over everything that I had gone through. I was looking for names to call him and her so I wouldn't use their real names. Trust me the names that I was coming up with was not pretty. I took a few minutes and shed a few tears because this was not me at all, I was a different person. I stopped writing and took some time off because I (me) could not write a book like that. After a few months' past, I decided to go back to the writing, but this time things were a little different.

I had taken the time to focus on what was at hand in my life at that time. I also had to search my heart to see if I was truly in a place to write about my situation and use my journal to recall the details. See my journal captured everything that went on during my separation and eventual divorce, but the book title came from an assignment that I had to write for my Bishop. His assignment was for me to write a sermon on Manifestation and waiting until it happens. I titled the sermon "While I Wait" and submitted the sermon to him and received great feedback on it. Thus, the title of my book While I'm Waiting!

Before starting again, I decided to take a different route. I decided to pray about it because I did not want to write an angry book, I wanted to write something that I could be proud of and something that would be real. I wanted someone to know that in any situation you're gonna go through it and it's not gonna always be roses. I want someone to know that you're not gonna always get it right, it's gonna hurt, it's ok to react, and it's ok to feel. As a Christian we are expected to be on this pedestal and be perfect because we love God, and we should always be "Christ like". Well, it doesn't always work that way and you should not have that much pressure on your shoulders. I had to pray a lot and ask Him for guidance, to teach me His way of doing this, and to help me to be better. I counted my birthing process as if I were really carrying a baby in my womb. I figured that certain levels was like the 3 trimesters: (1st trimester) The stress and anxiety and the grieving of the loss, (2nd trimester) Feeling a little relief, but the depression and the transition from all the blows and countless emotional rollercoasters, (3rd trimester) A little easier and acceptance that in no time this will soon be over and I could take joy in my expected end.

There is no BIG PUSH!!! I did not even realize that I had transitioned until sometime later. I wouldn't trade what I went through for anything in the world, don't get me wrong, I still at times miss my family the way that it was, but I am now in my new season of ME! I have grown and I am still growing, You would be surprised as to how we all get along. No, we are not one big happy family, but we can conversate with each other about the girls in a manner that would surprise you. I'm even shocked myself as to how far we have come. That lets you know that you have peace and you're in a different place in life. Some of my friends say that they couldn't do it, but I'm grateful to be the example. I have learned so much about who I am and what I need for me to be comfortable with myself. I'm even more humbled and grateful than I have ever been in my life and I am moving forward to greater things with my girls in tow. I'm Still Waiting!

Why Are You Waiting?

How Are You Waiting?

Made in the USA
Columbia, SC
18 February 2021